TAKE WHAT YOU WILL FROM THIS FOLKS!

Tales and stories from The Peoples Artist

SILENT BILL

Copyright © Silent Bill & SSOSVA 2019

ISBN: 9781792111648

No part of this book may be reproduced in any written, electronic, recording or photocopying without written permission of the author. Although every precaution has been taken to verify the accuracy of the information contained herein, the author assumes no responsibility for any errors or omissions. No liability is assumed for damages that may result from the use of information contained within.

Names, characters, businesses, places, events, locales, and incidents are either the products of the author's imagination or used in a fictitious manner. Any resemblance to actual persons, living or dead, or actual events is purely coincidental. Attempts have been made to credit anything that is referenced. In case of error, correction, referencing or updating being needed then informing the author will ensure a correction on the next available print. That's if you know how to find him.

Dedicated to Rachel Blu
The funniest person I know.

Introduction

I first began writing my 'As The Peoples Artist' posts on a Monday morning quite simply because Mondays sucked arse. The dreaded start to the week needed some form of light entertainment and low brow humour and I had so much shit in my head that needed to be put out somewhere. I never knew when I made my first post that I would continue 'As The People's Artist' for over three years, so its mental to think that it all began with this post:

Mondays and back to work are such a mood hoover so as The Peoples Artist it's my job to spread happiness on the drab back-to-work Mondays so here is my inspirational start to the week speech.

"By working your arse off for eight hours a day you may eventually get to become boss and get to work your arse off for twelve hours a day!!!!"

Granted my first post wasn't exactly Voltaire or Nietzsche and it didn't even have my signing off of 'Take what you will from this folks' but It was the start of something I'd come to enjoy doing every week.

I was shocked at how much others seemed to enjoy the posts as well, as when at art events and meeting new folk their first words weren't the usual "I thought you'd be taller" it started becoming comments about how they buzzed off 'The Peoples Artist' posts. The first few posts weren't spectacular but they gradually started to find their feet and become their own covering all manner of topics. Some are light-hearted, some serious, some true, some folklore and some are merely ramblings I wanted to get off my chest. The best ones tended to be the ambiguous posts that are open to interpretation and are read differently by various people, hence my closing line each week.

However, as with life, you can't please everyone and some may not see the tongue in cheek humour or necessarily even be open to any of the hidden meanings within the posts. It's no loss to me, they don't have to read it, however it is heartening to know that you aren't one of those people as you are reading this now. I hope you enjoy reading these pages but I must insist that it only be read on a Monday, if read on any other days then somewhere a unicorn dies (Allegedly).

Silent Bill

As The Peoples Artist it's my job on a Monday morning to remind you to be wary of offers too good to be true.

A man is getting into the shower just as his wife is finishing up her shower when the doorbell rings. The wife quickly wraps herself in a towel and runs downstairs. When she opens the door, there stands Dave, her husband's best mate. They've always got on well and had a good-humoured relationship so before she says a word, Dave says jokingly, "I'll give you £500 to drop that towel." After thinking for a moment how hilarious it would be, she drops her towel and stands laughing naked in front of Dave.

Dave goes into his pockets and takes out the £500 and leaves pissing himself laughing. The woman wraps back up in the towel and goes back upstairs. When she gets to the bathroom, her husband asks. "Who was that?"

"It was Dave" she replies. "Great!" the husband says, "Did he say anything about the £500 he owes me?"

Take what you will from this folks and have a good week.

As The Peoples Artist it's my job on a Monday morning to remind you that blowing out someone else's candle doesn't make yours shine any brighter.

An ingenious school teacher called Rosie Dutton used two apples to illustrate the effects of bullying to a room full of children. She talked about the apples and the children described how both apples were similar size but one was red and was one green. She picked up the red apple and dropped it on the floor telling the children how she hated this apple, and that it was disgusting, it was a horrible colour and the stem was just too short. She told them that because she didn't like it then she didn't want them to like it either, so they should call it names too.

The children took it in turns calling the red apple a name and dropping it on the floor, after they all had took turns doing this Miss Dutton cut both the apples open. The red apple that had been called names and dropped was bruised and all damaged inside.

The kids really understood it, the bruises and the fucked-up insides resonated with them. They could comprehend it. When kids are bullied, they feel fucked up inside and sometimes don't show or tell others how they are feeling. If they hadn't have cut that apple open, they'd not have known how much damage they had caused it.

Take what you will from this folks and have a good week.

As The Peoples Artist it's my job on a Monday morning to remind you that the person who does not think and plan long ahead will find trouble right at their door.

When I was 16 and had my first girlfriend and had just become sexually active so I practiced safe sex. There was awkwardness about disposing of condoms as I didn't want my mum seeing them so when I left the house to walk my girlfriend home I dropped them down the grid outside my house. This became my ritual for a few months.

One morning I awoke to find the whole road covered in multi coloured condoms, strewn all over the place, literally about 200 of them. It looked like some messed up art installation. My initial thought was "What dirty shit has thrown that many about in the street, why can't they put them down the grid like me". Then it hit me! it had rained super heavy for the few days prior and the grid must have filled up to the point that all condoms had risen up from the grid and had returned to haunt me. I was so paranoid I had to go out in the street and pick them all up. Oh the humanity.

Take what you will from this folks and have a good week.

As The Peoples Artist it's my job on a Monday morning to remind you that holding onto anger is like drinking poison and expecting the other person to die.

A native Indian grandfather was talking with his grandson and he says there are two wolves inside of us which are always at war with each other. One of them is a good wolf which represents things like kindness, forgiveness and love. The other is a bad wolf, which represents hate, resentment, and bitterness.

The grandson stops and thinks about it for a second then he looks up at his grandfather and says, "Grandfather, which one wins?". The grandfather quietly replies, the one that you feed!

Take what you will from this folks and have a good week.

As the Peoples Artist it's my job on a Monday morning to remind you that every piece of street art is a mini revolution.

Sometimes in life we as the little people don't really have a voice or a say on anything in the world, we vote and its overturned, we protest and we are arrested, we speak are minds and we are accused of being trouble makers (Or as John Doh likes to say 'Misunderstood') but the one platform we have to get our voices heard is via our art. Via our art we can raise awareness of things that may not reach other parts of the UK (And even the world), we shame councils into overturning Public Space Protection Orders, we raise money for good causes and charities, we highlight social injustices, we inspire people to have a go and join in.

Never forget that the piece you've done up somewhere might cheer someone up on their daily grind to work, it just might inspire someone to think "I wanna have a go at that', it might make someone think about the issue you are raising or mostly likely it will just have someone drawing a giant comedy cock over it.

Take what you will from this folks and have a good week.

As The Peoples Artist it's my job on a Monday morning to remind you what good is beauty if you are ugly inside?

I had the privilege the other week of listening to a motivational speech by the amazing and beautiful Katie Piper, who was attacked with acid by her ex-boyfriend and an accomplice, causing major damage to her face and blindness in one eye.

Her speech really struck with me not just about the human spirit but the way beauty is defined. She rightly spoke about how it's not appearance that defines us but the old cliché of beauty is skin deep, but who better to teach it to us than Miss Piper. She had no airs or graces about her, she had an amazing outlook on life, her sense of humour was on par with most comedians and she was a truly beautiful person.

Speaking from experience, the majority of people that I have encountered that are obsessed with self-image, appearance and vanity are narcissistic twats and really shitty human beings. In their minds they have a public image of themselves that actually doesn't correlate with their actual human interactions.

They think their appearance gives them a somewhat self-entitled grace about them.

Luckily for society they tend to gravitate towards one another and are left out of our mating pool. So, remember people, its beauty that attracts the eye but its personality that captures the heart.

Take what you will from this folks and have a good week.

I've just installed an electric fence in my back garden.

My neighbour is dead against it.

As The Peoples Artist it's my job on a Monday morning to remind you that you can be blind to the happiness right in front of you.

There once was a blind girl who hated her life because she was blind. She hated everyone, except her loving boyfriend. He was always there for her. She said that if she could only see the world then she would be truly happy. One day, someone donated a pair of eyes to her and when she awoke from the corneal operation she could see everything, including her boyfriend. Her boyfriend asked her, "Now that you can see the world, are you truly happy"

The girl was shocked when she saw that her boyfriend was blind too, and became angry at him and told him she was unhappier than when she was blind. The boyfriend utterly shocked, left and they never spoke again.

A few days later the girl received a letter from the boyfriend, the text was barely eligible but it simply read "Take care of my eyes dear."

Take what you will from this folks and have a good week.

As The Peoples Artist it's my job on a Monday morning to remind you that in the future everyone will be famous for 15 seconds.

Andy Warhol famously once "In the future, everyone will be world-famous for 15 minutes" but in today's age of vloggers, YouTubers and influencers it appears that kids these days no longer wish to be doctors, vets or astronauts, they all want to be famous.

With TV shows featuring Z listers dancing or eating kangaroo's bollocks there's a whole generation out there thinking they too will have some 15 minutes of fame. Not sure how this cycle will ever be broken when there's over a million videos on YouTube of people simply opening up kinder eggs... WTF have we become.

Take what you will from this folks and have a good week.

As The Peoples Artist it's my job on a Monday morning to remind you that there are somethings that money can't buy... like morals and integrity.

There was once a young single guy who lived at home with his elderly father. He worked at the family business and was set to inherit a fortune when his father passed away.

He knew his father didn't have long to live and wanted a wife to share his soon to be fortune with. One night he bumped into the most beautiful woman he had ever seen. He approached her and said "I may look like an ordinary fella but I'm due to inherit 100 million pounds in a few weeks when my father passes away.

The woman was very impressed and took his name and business card. A week later when she met him again she was his step mum.

Take what you will from this folks and have a good week.

As The Peoples Artist it's my job on a Monday morning to remind you that a smart person is one who can pretend to be an idiot in front of an idiot pretending to be smart.

As a kid I used to play on Street Fighter 2 arcade machine in a chippy by where I lived but the staff that worked there were absolute wankers. They would just generally be bell ends to all us kids that went in there to play the game. I never used to chat much simply just to avoid the incessant bullshit from them so they assumed I was stupid or something. They thought I was a simpleton and thought a little game they had going on to mock me was funny. Each time I went in there they would offer me 10p or a 50p for nothing so I could play the game. I would always take the 10p and play my game whilst they laughed amongst themselves assuming I was thick as shit.

I did this every time until one day I went and the arcade game was no longer there. One of the staff there commented on how stupid I was that I never ever took the 50p.

They thought that they were clever but I thanked them for the countless free games I had there and told them that the moment I ever did take the 50p not the 10p then my game with them would be up.

Take what you will from this folks and have a good week.

As The Peoples Artist it's my job on a Monday morning to remind you that you can't please everyone in this life.

I'm realising more and more and that trying to please everyone is an impossibility but trying to piss people off is really piss-easy. Sometimes no matter what you do, you will somehow cause upset unintentionally to someone. They will think you have somehow wronged them and make you feel like shit when you have literally done nothing wrong.

Aristotle once said that in order to avoid criticism then do nothing, say nothing and be nothing. I think he has a point as you cannot change how or what they think or say but you can control how you respond and I think that's when Aristotle's words ring true, simply say nothing. You cannot argue or reason and please everyone.

Take what you will from this folks and have a good week.

As The Peoples Artist it's my job on a Monday morning to remind you that it's not enough to have lived, you should be determined to live for something.

Recently my mother was diagnosed with a rarer form of cancer, and mums being mums (Well my mum) her motto was simply "Business as usual". She was happy and content knowing she had raised her children and saw her grandchildren. I could see her way of thinking but there was more left for her and more future grandchildren for her to see.

She's always been a trooper and not one to just give in. She never once complained or moaned and had the right mental attitude to face this. She was even under pressure from the usual life woes as well such as rent and bills yet she motored on. The family barely spoke of it other than when one of us would say "she's a proper hard bastard" or "she's a fuckin trooper" as all my family know what my mums like.

Miraculously my mum got the all clear a few months back and is recovering well. I know 100% that it was her attitude and mental state that contributed to this.

There was more left for her to live for, that I can only guess at but it's taught me that we all should be determined to live for something whatever it is we choose and that the purpose of life is a life of purpose.

So, if you know a family member or a friend going through this now then please share this story of hope with them.

Take what you will from this folks and have a good week.

As The Peoples Artist it's my job on a Monday morning to remind you that there is no past, there is no future, there is only the here and now.

We spend our whole lives worrying about either past events that we can't change or future events that are yet to happen yet we only have control over two moments in our lives, the here and now. Fuck everything that has gone before, all our times are now here in the present, that is all we need. I'm not talking all spiritual or mindful stuff just the essential essence of being you, who you are, flaws an all but right now here in the present. Don't even worry about the future as a very wise and spiritual person I know once told me "life has a way of giving you what it needs", and you know what, I think they are right.

Take what you will from this folks and have a good week.

NB - All level 2 Time Travellers pay no attention to this post.

I could have sworn I just saw Michael J. Fox
in the local garden centre…

I can't be sure though as he had his back to the fuchsias.

As The Peoples Artist it's my job on a Monday morning to remind you that sometimes the only answer people are looking for when they ask for help is that they won't have to face the problem alone.

Some people will offer all manner of logical solutions to your problems yet the only thing that can power you through the darkness back into the light is those around you that love, care and respect you. The people you love just being around in your time of need is the only answer needed. You know who they are when that time arrives and that feeling can overcome any obstacle. (That will and a bit of Stan Bush).

"Sometimes when your hopes have all been shattered
And there's nowhere to turn, you wonder how you keep going
Think of all the things that really mattered, And the chances you've earned,

The fire in your heart is growing
You can fly, if you try, leaving the past behind
Heaven only knows what you might find

Dare, dare to believe you can survive, you hold the future in your hands,

Dare, dare to keep all of your dreams alive
It's time to take a stand, and you can win, if you dare

Everybody's trying to break your spirit, keeping you down
Seems like it's been forever,
But there's another voice if you'll just hear it, Saying it's the last round,
Looks like it's now or never
Out of the darkness you stumble into the light, Fighting for the things you know are right."

Stan Bush - Dare

(From the original Transformers Movie, Animated Version)

Take what you will from this folks and have a good week.

As The Peoples Artist it's my job on a Monday morning to remind you that reality is merely an illusion, albeit a persistent one.

Yesterday after a hard day's vandalising in another city I returned home too early and Baby Bill had deadlocked the door. I text a mate to see if he was up and luckily, he had partied all night and hadn't been to bed yet but was just going. He told me he would leave the door on the latch and to help myself to a brew and a munch.

I arrived at his and made a brew and ate a brownie off a plate in the fridge. I stayed there for half an hour then it became apparent that the brownies were special brownies. For those that attended my solo art show last month, you know what I mean.

First, I rode the highs laughing at my surreal thoughts of a unicorn shitting my name in the sand to the paranoia lows of twitching the curtains looking out the window for the vandal police.

I later returned home wondering if every person I passed could tell I was smashed and I was literally sweating saw dust. I got in and had the worst case of feather mouth and the munchies but sat for 30 minutes pondering Malthusian economics.

I retreated to bed and watched The Apprentice but for a whole hour I heard music coming from Baby Bills room which sounded like one song on continuous loop and when I text her asking if the same song was on a loop she replied that she wasn't even playing any music.

I learnt a lesson about eating potential psychoactive foodstuffs yesterday... I should have eaten two brownies instead of just the one.

Take what you will from this folks and have a good week.

.

As The Peoples Artist it's my job on a Monday morning to remind you that knowing what it feels like to be in pain is the reason we try to be kind to others.

A man and his young teenage son checked in to a hotel and were shown to their room. The receptionists noted the quiet manner of the guests, and the pale appearance of the boy. Later the man and boy ate dinner in the hotel restaurant. The staff again noticed that the two guests were very quiet and disheartened. After eating, the boy went to his room and the man went to reception and asked to see the manager.

The man explained that he was spending the night in the hotel with his fourteen-year-old son, who was terminally ill. His son was due to have therapy, which would cause him to lose his hair. They had come to the hotel to have a break together, and also because the boy planned to shave his head, that night, rather than feel that the illness was beating him.

The father said that he would be shaving his own head too, in support of his son. He asked that staff be respectful when the two of them came to breakfast with their shaved heads. The manager assured the father that he would inform all staff and that they would behave appropriately.

The following morning the father and son entered the restaurant for breakfast. There they saw the four male restaurant staff attending to their duties, perfectly normally, all with shaved heads.

Take what you will from this folks and have a good week.

As The Peoples Artist it's my job to remind you once again that some days you're the pigeon and some days you're the statue.

I have mentioned this before in the past but it's the one constant in our lives that we need reminding of. We will have periods where we are the pigeon flying high, shitting down on life and then there will be periods of us being the ones getting shat upon. It's almost part of the universe, like gravity. I have seen mates go through days, weeks, and even months at their lowest ebbs knowing and willing that they rise miraculously, just like the price of bitcoin (And fall again).

It's like that wise man once said, "That life is a roller coaster" was it Aristotle? or maybe Confucius who said this? Well anyways, I digress, but you just have to accept and enjoy both the ups and the downs, enjoy the downs you might say? Yes, because you won't be there forever and I know that if you are here reading this then you are one of life's fighters and you won't stay down forever.

So as hard as it seems then enjoy the downs, taking the little wins, share them with friends, let us revel in your triumphs and also share the woes, let us gently give you a kick you up the arse when you need it.

Take what you will from this folks and have a good week.

*Me toddles off singing "Life is a rollercoaster, Just gotta ride it"

As The Peoples Artist it's my job on a Monday morning to remind you that there are those that tell you it can't be done, but you are the one to get that job done.

"Somebody said that it couldn't be done, But he with a chuckle replied That maybe it couldn't, but he would be one Who wouldn't say so "till he tried."
So he buckled right in with the trace of a grin on his face.
If he worried, he hid it.He started to sing as he tackled the thing
That couldn't be done, and he did it.

Somebody scoffed: "Oh, you'll never do that; At least no one ever has done it."
But he took off his coat and took off his hat
And the first thing he knew he'd begun it.
With the lift of his chin and a bit of a grin,
Without any doubting or quiddit,
He started to sing as he tackled the thing
That couldn't be done, and he did it.

There are thousands to tell you it cannot be done, There are thousands to prophesy failure;
There are thousands to point out to you, one by one,
The dangers that wait to assail you.

But just buckle right in with a bit of a grin,
Then take off your coat and go to it;

Just start in to sing as you tackle the thing
That cannot be done, and you'll do it"

Edgar A. Guest

Take what you will from this folks and have a good week.

As The Peoples Artist it's my job on Monday morning to remind you that whatever troubles you are going through, there is someone, somewhere worse off.

Everyone in life has their troubles and the past few months for me have been difficult. If it's taught me anything though it's that whilst we can have a moan about the shit going on in our lives, there are people out there dealing with things of a much greater severity. Take a step back and assess your situation and think of those having a much harder time and like them stay strong and keep the faith.

Take what you will from this folks and have a good week.

As The Peoples Artist it's my job on a Monday morning to remind you that to truly think outside the box you must actually be off your box.

My dad is a mentalist and truly comes up with thinking outside the box solutions, albeit never within normal everyday situations.

My dad was on lads' holiday in Germany on the piss and they all like casual wear and spotted a shop with Fred Perry stuff etc. They are all Scallys (a roguish self-assured young person) and even though they are grown men they act like teens and like to steal. In order to break into the shop my dad came up with an ingenious idea and took them all to a hardware store which they broke into to get the tools to break into the clothes shop!

Later on, they were at an all you can drink bar but they were drinking the place dry so management asked them to leave. They all refused and it started to get a bit out of hand and doors were locked to stop them leaving with bouncers bringing out shooters. My dad in all his wisdom grabs one of his mates, throws him out the window, smashing it so they can all climb out.

They all clamber out and the fella that my dad had thrown through the glass actually turns to my dad while running away and says "Thanks for that, we could have been shot".

When my dad first recanted this tale to me I said "Dad, why did you throw your mate through the window" and he said "Its fuckin obvious, so we could get out" so I then asked "Why not throw a chair through the window?" He just stared at me blankly like the thought had never even crossed his mind.

Take what you will from this folks and have a good week.

I was asked to describe myself in 3 words…Lazy

Comme The Peoples Artiste , il est mon travail sur un lundi matin pour vous rappeler que rien ne vaut avoir été jamais réalisé sans effort .

Vivimos en una lo quiero ahora generación con todo ser alimentados con cuchara para nosotros. Si todo fue fácil en la vida entonces todos estaríamos haciendo, se necesita tiempo , esfuerzo y recursos para lograr cualquier cosa de cualquier mérito.

Du musst weitermachen und ausharren

Take what you will from this folks and have a good week.

As the Peoples Artist it is my job on a Monday morning to remind you that whilst as one person we cannot change the world, however we can change the world of one person.

I got chatting to a homeless person the other day and was astounded when they told me that he hadn't spoken to a person in 2 weeks, can you imagine no human interaction for 2 whole weeks? He said me stopping to speak to him had made his day and restored his faith in humanity. His faith however was short lived when I asked him "Do you know what's the biggest cause of homeless people's deaths"

He thought for a second then said "cold weather"

I then donned my balaclava and whilst rooting in my bag as I menacingly said "Wrong...It's my hammer".

Of course, I'm joking (I said "My Axe") but it just goes to show how as one single person I know we can't change the world, but we can however change the world of one person. So when out and about next, do something nice for someone.

Take what you will from this folks and have a good week.

As The Peoples Artist it's my job on a Monday morning to remind just how many unhinged individuals there are on social media.

In my short time on here I have encountered my fair share of The Crazies (Haven't we all) but more recently there has been surge of them. They vary from the "Not the smartest peanut in the turds" to the "Noam Chomsky readers and the intelligentsia".

Every one of them I've encountered suffers from delusions of grandeur (but don't all us artists) and has a very high and unwarranted opinion of themselves. All engagement with these folk tends to mood hoover any of the fun I derive from my art life. Sometimes being nice and an open-minded human being actually becomes a detriment to your own mental well-being as these people just don't actually realise what a nuisance and stress they actually are.

So, on that note, let me apologise if I am one of them.

Take what you will from his folks and have a good week.

As The Peoples Artist it is my job on a Monday morning to remind you that when love is not madness then it is not love.

How does one describe love? Is it waking and first thought is of them? Is it they are your last thought at night? Is it the constant checking of the phone for messages? Being drove crazy but in an amazing way is the most strangest feeling I have ever experienced. It's both scary and exciting at the same time and is summed up by a phrase by Nietzsche who once said that you must have chaos within you to give birth to a dancing star.

Chaos is not the word though, I don't think there is even a word to describe it. Feeling so alive yet so fragile and vulnerable. So happy one minute then fraught the next. It truly is one of life's amazing experiences. However, the saddest most awful truth you will come to find is the people that make you feel this way are not the ones with whom we get to spend our lives.

But the love we cannot have is the one that lasts the longest, hurts the deepest and feels the strongest.

Take what you will from his folks and have a good week.

As The Peoples Artist it's my job on a Monday morning to remind you to know your worth and never settle for less than you deserve.

There is an old story of a boilermaker who was hired to fix a huge steamship boiler system that had broken down. After listening to the engineer's description of the problems he went to the boiler room. He looked at the maze of twisting pipes, listened to the thump of the boiler and the hiss of escaping steam for a few minutes, and felt some pipes with his hands. Then he hummed softly to himself, reached into his overalls and took out a small hammer, and tapped a bright red valve, once.

Immediately the entire system began working perfectly, and the boilermaker went home. When the steamship owner received a bill for £1,000 he complained that the boilermaker had only been in the engine room for five minutes, and requested an itemized bill. This is what the boilermaker sent him:

For tapping with hammer: £0.50
For knowing where to tap: £999.50
Total: £1,000.00

Take what you will from this folks and have a good week.

As The Peoples Artist it's my job on a Monday morning to remind you to trust your gut instincts.

Scientists have discovered that our first decision is usually the right one, which I agree with.

Take this for example when I was a teenager I had a best mate Danny and we had hung around together all the time. We did everything together, went concerts, dropped acid, bunked school, chased tail and had a good ole time. One day when bunking school Danny confessed to me that he preferred The Rolling Stones over the Beatles!

I got up and left and I never spoke to him ever again. I discovered the other day that he is now in prison for murder. Trust your instincts folks.

Take what you will from this folks and have a good week.

I went into the library today and was mistaken for a library assistant by an old lady who asked me for a book on innuendo.

So I took her up the rear aisle and gave her one!!

As The Peoples Artist it is my job on a Monday morning to make you all feel better about the weekend's hangovers (And ale paranoia).

Jesus apparently claimed to have turned water into wine (No evidence) yet I managed to turn the whole of my months wage into Morgan's Spiced Rum (Evidenced), so I say your turn Jesus!

I'd like to say that work drives me to drink but I wouldn't like to have to thank them for the pleasure and in all honesty I fuckin love it. Being drunk allows me the one time to chat to complete strangers, think I'm great on karaoke, make amazing plans for art that I forget in the morning, hell even have a lie down in the street if it takes my fancy (perhaps a lil snooze also). Who cares if you have to wake up and first check your actually at home in your own bed, then check for any spray paint you may have done on your living room walls, finally checking what shit you've posted on Facebook.

I say Hail the ale and worship the wine. Roll on the weekend.

Take what you will from this folks and have a good week.

As The Peoples Artist it's my job on a Monday morning to remind you to strap in tight for the roller coaster that is life.

Within life you have to accept that some days you are the pigeon, and some days you are the statue. Albeit days as the statue you just hope someone at least puts a traffic cone on your head!

Life is meant to be ups and downs and a bit of a struggle, without the bitter we'd never be able to appreciate the sweet. You just have to accept the ups as your little victories and when the downs approach brace yourself ready for the next climb.

Just remember though folks it's up to you whether you scream and shit yourself on the drop down or throw your hands up and enjoy it!

Take what you will from this folks and have a good week. *

* To my sadist/masochist friends I hope you have a shit week.

As The Peoples Artist it's my job on a Monday morning to remind you all just how much we are the real rebels.

You read about rich rock stars being rebels but it's us normal folk that are the real rebels, each in our own way. We are the ones who tell the TV Licence man to fuck off, we are the ones who have pillow fights in the street, we are the ones risking prosecution stickering and stenciling, we are the ones supporting each other online, we march to our own drums. So please continue in your rebel ways.

Take what you will from this folks and have a good week.

As The Peoples Artist it's my job on a Monday Morning to remind you to get ready for tomorrow, today.

Every morning around the world a street artist wakes up. They know they must be smarter and run faster than the fastest policeman or they will be caught. Every morning a policeman wakes up. They know they must outrun and outsmart the slowest street artist or they will be beaten.

It doesn't matter whether you are the street artist or the policeman. When the sun comes up, you'd better be ready.

Take what you will from this folks and have a good week.

THESAURUS FOR SALE

Brand new, current, fresh, mint condition, modern, new-fangled, original, pristine, recent, spotless, untapped, untouched, untried, unused.

If Interested call 0800-SilentBill

As The Peoples Artist it's my job on a Monday to remind you to love thy neighbour as thyself.

Mind you I have some right shits for neighbours. My next-door neighbour knocked on my door at 3 in the morning. Can you fuckin believe that? 3:00 AM! Lucky for him I was still up playing my bagpipes!

The feminist to the other side of me, her garden is a proper mess; her bush is really overgrown round the front. The couple opposite me also like to have sex so we can all see. If I climb on my wardrobe and squeeze in the gap between the ceiling and use my binoculars I can just about peep through the curtains.

I wouldn't mind but its them cheeky shits that keep knocking at mine an all to tell me to either put some clothes on or buy curtains. The nerve of some people.

Take what you will from this folks and have a good week.

As The Peoples Artist it's my job on a Monday morning to remind you all that the grass isn't always greener on the other side.

In the past I've seen people and I have been envious of their lives thinking that I have somehow gone wrong in my own life. I've seen them with their fancy cars, owning their own home and have what appear to be great lifestyles only to later find out that they are miserable, they are splitting up with their partners, have addictions and they are totally washed up.

It comes as somewhat of a shock to later find out that they were actually envious of my life and how happy I am with it. This led me to think that if the grass looks greener on the other side, you can almost guarantee that it's covered in shit.

So, I leave you with this, just be happy with your life and being you and if you're not then do something about it.

Take what you will from this folks and have a good week.

As The Peoples Artist it's my job on a Monday to remind you all take some time out to reflect and have some chill time.

After missing a flight to Spain for a SSOSVA exhibition, turning up a day late it made me realise that sometimes you can just be running on 'auto-pilot' and doing too much. I work 6 days a week in a very stressful environment and I'm also on call for 3 nights of the week. I also have the usual family commitments as well as extended family commitments.

I know a lot of you are in very similar situations as me and I often wonder how we find the time for our creative pursuits. Which brings me to the Art, the one saving grace amongst all this pressure and basically what I use to chill. I thank you all for making this part of my life a very happy and rewarding experience and long may it continue.

Take what you will from this folks and have a good week.

As The Peoples Artist it's my job on a Monday morning to remind you that the only competition in life is yourself.

When I first began making art it was within the genre of money art and in my naivety, I wanted to be the best. I soon realised that my skill set and knowledge of art at the time wouldn't allow that so I had to simply become the best that I could be. However, don't let that stop you from telling people you are the best because if you can't convince yourself you're the best then how are you going to convince others you are.

Furthermore, too many people within the urban art scene see their whole art journey as some kind of competition, which in the long term is counterproductive and eventually self-destructive. They spend too much time concerned with what others appear to be doing, seeing it as competition when in reality there actually is no competition. We are all in this together, so just simply be the best you can.

Take what you will from this folks and have a good week.

As The Peoples Artist it's my job on a Monday morning to remind you that an eye for an eye will only make the whole world blind.

One of my mates' brothers was a totally arsehole to my mate and one weekend we happened up on the chance to administer retribution and revenge upon him. Their Mum was going away for the night with their Nan and Granddad to London and their Mum had made him and his brother a pan of Scouse (Stew) to for tea that night.

Being the unhinged little shits that we were, we spotted the opportunity and decided to spike the pan of Scouse with Magic Mushrooms to freak his brother out. After spiking the scouse, it was all going to plan so imagine our horror when their Mum, Nan and Grandad returned as the car had broken down, cancelling the trip and proceeded to join in eating the scouse.

We both thought 'In for a penny in for a pound' so we joined in the festivities and ate the Scouse also. The night proceeded to be something that I will never forget. During the 'Party' I went the toilet and returned telling everyone how I didn't fall off the toilet and how I didn't invent the wait for it… FUCKS CAPACITOR…What was going on in my warped 'Back to The Future' mind?

The highlight of the night for me was his Nan raving to Oceanic "Dream Tripper" and his Granddad telling us convincingly that he had invented the banana.

Take what you will from this folks and have a good week.

What's the most offensive C word in the English language?

Cancer...

It's a Cunt!

As The Peoples Artist it's my job on a Monday morning to remind you that quick thinking can literally save your skin (Your Banana Skin).

When I was about 10 years of age I went through a phase of stealing, I'd steal unwanted or unneeded items just for the hell of it (I once stole tampons!!!!). Well anyway, back to the story. For some odd reason me and a friend was in the local Fruit & Veg shop and we decided to steal bananas and oranges. We were both hardly Adam Worth so naturally we both got caught by the shopkeeper who took us to the back-stockroom cupboard and locked us in whilst he went to ring the police.

This was the 80's before mobile phones and CCTV and nowadays we could probably get him arrested for kidnapping but anyways were in a stock cupboard wondering how to get out of the predicament. There are no windows to climb out of and there are only boxes in the stockroom. My mate was ready to cry when I came up with the ingenious idea of eating the evidence. I ate 3 bananas and the skin and I made my mate eat the oranges and the peel. It was brutal but when needs must.

The shop keeper eventually returned with the police and we were both sat there with massive shit eating grins on our faces, my mate stank of oranges but like I said this was the days before

CCTV and they had to let us go. I often look back on the idea of eating the evidence and to this day I think thank fuck we never stole the pineapples and coconuts.

Take what you will from this folks and have a good week.

As The Peoples Artist it's my job on a Monday morning to remind you that saying nothing sometimes says the most.

Take what you will from this folks and have a good week.

As The Peoples artist it's my job on a Monday morning to remind you to be grateful for what you already have.

Anyone that's purchased a home will know that home buying is stressful. Every letter and phone call regarding it brings more bad news of both time and expense, both of which people cannot afford. The landlord is selling the house I currently rent so we have to get out and the home we are buying requires extra work which is looking likely we cannot afford. Even though this is totally stressing me I count myself lucky that we've still got a roof over our heads that we would be able to afford to rent somewhere else if this goes tits up.

Last year alone there were 53,000 households that were accepted by local authorities as homeless and in priority need. 35,969 were households with dependent children. I can't imagine the position these families must be in and it breaks my heart even thinking about it. So, remember to be grateful for what you already have.

Take what you will from this folks and have a good week.

As The Peoples Artist it's my job on a Monday morning to remind you that laughter is the best medicine.

Mark Twain once said "Against the assault of laughter nothing can stand" which I tend to agree with. However, there are exceptions, for example when I arrive home at 5 in the morning smashed out my tits laughing and can't even stand.

Even the shittiest of days can be salvaged with a good old laugh. There are friends of mine that can say a phrase or sentence that completely creases me and cheers me up beyond all belief. People cheering me up and making me laugh is probably the best gift they could give me other than money, beer or sex.

So anyone that wants to feed me beer whilst fucking me and telling me jokes at the same and also willing to pay me for the privilege then I'd be extremely cheered up (NB: Only females need apply). Oh, one last thing, if you find yourself laughing for no apparent reason then perhaps it's actually medication that you need.

Take what you will from this folks and have a good week.

As The Peoples Artist it's my job on a Monday to remind you that life experience is the art of drawing sufficient conclusions from insufficient evidence.

For example, I had noticed recently that I had been returning home on numerous occasions to find the kitchen stinking of cigarettes and my beers missing. Having a teenage daughter (Baby Bill), I naturally accused her which she vehemently denied. Having the paradox of totally trusting my daughter yet having a paranoid personality disorder I decided I'd set up a camera in the kitchen to capture on film this apparent magic portal that was consuming my beers.

What I discovered blew my mind. When we had been going out our dog Zuki had been inviting round her other doggy pals to drink beers, smoke cigarettes and play poker. It turns out that me jumping to conclusions and not trusting my daughter was unwarranted, the camera did however reveal she is stealing the winning poker money from our dog Zuki's wallet whilst she's' asleep to fund her anarchist uprising.

Take what you will from this folks and have a good week.

As The Peoples Artist it's my job on a Monday morning to remind you to be wary of wolves in sheep's clothing.

Yesterday I was walking past a young lad selling newspapers and heard him shouting

"Be wary, con artist in the area, 61 people scammed".

This aroused my attention so I went and bought a newspaper from the kid. Upon closer inspection I noticed that not only was there no news of a con artist but it was also yesterday's newspaper.

I said angrily to the kid "You conning little shit, this is yesterday's paper"

He nonchalantly looked the other way and shouted "Be wary, con artist in the area, 62 people scammed"!

Take what you will from this folks and have a good week.

As The Peoples Artist it's my job to remind you that you can't please everyone, you have simply got to please yourself.

Try as you may to keep everyone happy within your art life and projects, its simply not going to happen. I remember a quote I heard Ozzy say when I was a kid about if you don't like his music then it's not for you, that's my stance with my life. If you don't like me or my art and find it silly what I or my peers do then it's simply not for you.

Most people will be polite and courteous if something isn't to their liking whilst there is always a small minority of people that will want to belittle and discredit what you do, some are even simply offended by words you use. Some people can't be pleased by anything and just love to hate, that's when you should apply the "My Haters are my Motivators" approach. Simply carry on with doing what makes you happy with even more vigour than before.

With that in mind, I will leave you with lyrics from Crazy Train by Ozzy.
"Maybe, it's not too late to learn how to love and forget how to hate."

Take what you will from this folks and have a good week.

As The Peoples Artist it's my job on a Monday morning to remind you that the word politics is derived from the word poly for many and ticks as in parasites.

When I was a kid I asked my dad to explain politics to me and he said "Look at it this way, I'm the breadwinner in the house so let's call me Capitalism. Your mum looks after the money so we'll call her the Government and as were both here to take care of you we'll call you the People. Your mum's friend (who was living with us at the time due to a divorce), we'll consider her the Working Class and your baby brother, we'll call him the Future. He told me to have a think about it to see if made sense.

I went to bed thinking about what my dad had told me and later that night I was woken up by my baby brother crying. I went to inspect him and he had totally shat his nappy, I mean caked in it as he had proper farted mud. I went to my mum and dads' room but my mum was asleep so I went to my mum's friend room. I opened the door and my dad was knobbing her. I thought fuck me, this isn't good so I quietly shut the door and went back to bed.

The next morning, I was a bit quiet and my dad asked me to tell him in my own words what I thought politics was all about. So, I told him "Well, while Capitalism is fucking the Working Class the Government is sound asleep, the People are being ignored and the Future is in deep shit.

Take what you will from this folks and have a good week.

As The Peoples Artist it's my job on a Monday morning to remind you that those that touch our lives will live in our hearts forever.

As a teenager I had a mate, Taylor. He was slightly older than me but he was cool as fuck. We hung out together taking acid, smoking weed, doodling, listening to metal albums, he taught me basic guitar riffs and we had some mad adventures. As I got older and I put away childish things but Taylor carried on. He was always nuttier than a squirrel's turd and sadly he gradually mentally declined and became involved in heavy drugs. He took his own life a few years back which left a void in my life, an emptiness that can't be replaced. I think of Taylor often and I am moved to tears knowing that if he was here today he would have been in The Secret Society of Super Villain Artists, making art and having a laugh with all of us.

Taylor, I love and miss you so much and you are always in my thoughts and my heart.

Take what you will from this folks and have a good week.

I can't stand people who don't know the difference between your and you're.

Their idiots

As The Peoples Artist it's my job on a Monday morning to remind you all that old age and deception will overcome youth and skill.

A few years back one of my previous job roles was in Tenancy Support helping people to live independently. An arsehole of a workmate who was very unemphatic and thought he knew it all supported a lovely old dear whom I shall refer to as Mrs. Morgan.

When he would visit Mrs. Morgan, upon leaving she would give my colleague a bag of almonds. Strictly speaking we are not allowed to take gifts but my colleague always took and ate them. He supported Mrs. Morgan for about 4 months till sadly she passed away peacefully in her sleep.

I attended the funeral and got chatting to a health visitor that was also supporting her towards the end of her life. The health visitor was saying how lovely she was and that she used to visit weekly and took her a bag of chocolate covered almonds every week. I thought chocolate covered almonds, chocolate covered almonds…

Fuck…Then it hit me…. She'd only been sucking the chocolate off the nuts and keeping the almonds to give to my colleague who must have been a twat to her. I never ever told my colleague about this and it still makes me laugh to this day. Mrs. Morgan, I salute you.

Take what you will from this folks and have a good week.

(Just don't go taking almonds off old dears)

As The Peoples Artist it's my job on a Monday morning to remind you that some mysteries are best left unsolved.

When I was a teenager my Grandad passed away so a few of the family left home and went to live with our Nan. There's was like 6 of us in a 4-bed roomed house and after being there about 4 months, I came across what I aptly named "The Phantom Logger".

This was simply the biggest turd I'd ever seen. Because there was a toilet upstairs and down Id discourage people from flushing it just so I could show more of my mates, I was considering charging it rent at one point. After a few weeks the initial buzz died down and normality resumed till 'The Phantom Logger' struck again. This time even bigger and broader than before. I refused to let anyone flush this one and I got about 4 days' worth of hard laughing out of it till it sadly was flushed away.

We couldn't work out which family member was doing this and we spent months speculating and investigating but never got any leads. Just as we would forget about it all of a sudden, we'd be gifted with what could only be described as the funniest massive turds you could ever imagine.

For 2 whole years the mysterious Phantom Logger stalked our bathrooms and to this day I still don't know who it was and secretly hoping that one day they may come out of retirement for one last push.

Take what you will from this folks and have a good week.

As The Peoples Artist it's my job on a Monday to remind you that 'He who dares wins'.

When I was a kid my Grandad recanted a story of when he worked on the docks. Back in the day it was commonplace for everyone that worked on the docks to find it totally acceptable to steal items from work in a roguish Del Boy manner.

My Grandad told me there was this one fella that was leaving the yard pushing a wheelbarrow full of soil. The security guard stopped him and naturally suspecting there were items buried in the soil made him tip it out. There was nothing in the wheelbarrow but soil and he shovelled back in and left. The very next day the same thing again, he is asked to tip it out, once again there's nothing hidden in the soil. At this point the security guard realises that this is a ruse to lull him into lowering his wits and that the next day's load will contain the stolen goods. The next day, the same game of wits was repeated and once again there was nothing in the soil.

This went on for 3 weeks then the man stopped and when the security guard asked him "why no soil?" he simply replied that his allotment was now finished. A few months later the security guard was in a pub and spotted the man and went over and asked him off the record, man to man "Come on, something was going on, what was you stealing?"

My Grandad said, the man took a sip of his pint, smiled and said "The wheelbarrows".

Take what you will from this folks and have a good week.

As The Peoples Artist it's my job on a Monday morning to remind you that you work to live, not live to work.

I'm from a normal working-class background and have watched my Mum and Nan work very hard all their lives with very little reward or other than the monetary value from it. My mum at some points when I was growing up worked 3 jobs. I know we all have the necessary evil of having to go to work but there has to be some reason behind it other than just getting by and paying the bills. I didn't want to fall into this trap so I have tried to spend the past few years doing mad shit, meeting amazing people and going mad places. Stuff as a lad from a council estate I would never really have thought possible. I urge anyone reading this to do the same, save up a little for that trip of a lifetime, visit a festival, a theatre visit, a nice meal, hell, whatever it is you will derive some enjoyment from. Start living people and remember you work to live, not vice versa.

Take what you will from this folks and have a good week.

As The Peoples Artist it's my job on a Monday morning to remind you that whilst logic will get you from A to Z; imagination will get you everywhere.

When I was younger Id pretend that our flight of stairs in the house was a mountain and I'd sit on each step for approximately 30 – 40 minutes before Id attempt to climb to the next step. I'd take a pack lunch with me and would have it when I was half way up the stairs with just my imagination to entertain me on my trek. Now as an adult I can't comprehend what I must have been thinking, I mean come on people, I was 15 years of age.

Also, after watching Willy Wonka and seeing the lick able flavoured wallpaper I couldn't wait to go to my Nan's house as she had wallpaper with grapes on and I so wanted to rush there to lick them. I ran all the way there burst the door down and headed right to the kitchen and proceeded to lick the grape wallpaper…it tasted like cigarette smoke. I still often find myself sitting on stairs thinking, pondering ideas and I still occasionally indulge in a random wall paper lick.

Take what you will from this folks and have a good week.

I used to date a girl with Eczema… Cracking tits!

As The Peoples Artist it's my job on a Monday morning to remind you that to quiet the mind is to ease the soul.

I went for lunch yesterday with my work wife who is very spiritual and we were chatting about alternative healings, which reminded me of the time I attended a meditation session. At first, I was apprehensive sitting bare foot in a darkened room with tree huggers who during the meditation fell into such a relaxed state that their diet of beans and pulses caused them to fart like crazy. I too also fell into a very deep relaxed state (without the farting might I add) and I swear my mind was took somewhere else and was at peace and completely empty.

After it finished I went to gather my trainers and as I looked over all the other shoes I couldn't spot mine and I thought that one of the hippies had taken off with them (In reality my feet stink that bad that my trainers run off on their own). I'm looking for mine and I spot a pair of Adidas that I thought were smart and made a mental note to myself to buy a pair of them. I was baffled as to where my trainers where so I went and asked the person who I paid the money to for the session. They looked at me like I was mental and pointed at the Adidas that I'd been admiring!

I was mind blown, how on earth was my mind that emptied that I didn't even recognise my own trainers? I felt such a knob that I denied they were mine and said mine had been stolen and had to walk home bare foot. I walked 2 miles home so if anyone tells you to quiet the mind is to ease the soul, they aren't talking about the soles of their feet coz mine were killing me.

Take what you will from this folks and have a good week.

As The Peoples Artist it's my job on a Monday morning to remind you that if 3 or more friends of yours are nutters then you probably are to.

Throughout my life I've hung around with some right hilarious crazy fuckers (I won't mention any names) and I've often wondered if I'm a mental magnet and I attract nutters. One mate of mine who worked in a key shop/cobblers, we would save our security tags from DVDs (The little silver sticky things) and he would put them in the soles of people's shoes when he re-heeled them so every time they entered shops they'd set alarms off and would have a clue why!

Another mate of mine was caught bollocko in Tesco car park doing wheel spins at 2 in the morning. It transpired he was working on a building site as security, got pissed up and for some reason he drove smashing though the locked security gates, when I asked him why he did it he replied "It's like in the films innit, I've always wanted to do it".

One of my best mates was taking his boss (A CEO of IT Company) out to strip clubs and high-end knocking shops however unbeknown to the boss my mate was using the company's corporate card (Whacked about 25 k on it). When he was found out my mate told the boss to get fucked as he couldn't do fuck all because he also would have been blown up to his missus for visiting knocking shops.

My craziest mate is someone who if he was pissed off with people he had a penchant for filling the kettle with water and taking a shit in it, knowing that they'd feel the kettle was full and would just boil it (Oh the humanity!). So take a look at your friends and if they get up to shit like this, rest assured there probably telling all their mates the crazy shit that you get up to also, referring to you as the nutter of the gang.

Take what you will from this folks and have a good week.

As The Peoples Artist it's my job on a Monday morning to remind you that sometimes we wear so many masks that we forget who we are underneath them.

>
> She had blue skin
> And so did he
> He kept it hid
>
> And so did she
> They searched for Blue
> Their whole life through
> Then passed each other
> And never knew
>
> By Shel Silverstein

Take what you will from this folks and have a good week.

As The Peoples Artist it's my job on a Monday morning to remind you that sticks and stones may break your bones but names can almost starve someone to death.

Whilst in high school I witnessed the power of words and the destruction that they can inflict upon a person. There was this one girl in my year, she was lovely and had the nicest demeanor and personality that anyone could wish for. She had the most amazing sense of humour ever and could find the joy out of the littlest things. I used to love chatting in the lessons that we had together however she was liked by all that knew her, however, she was tormented over her weight by the school bully.

The torment carried on throughout her time at school and it wasn't until recently I saw her again and she had changed since school and lost a load of weight. She had transformed herself and looked completely different. I mentioned to my mate in the pub Id saw her and how well she looked and had lost a lot of weight. My mate told me that she was in fact not physically well at all as she had struggled with eating disorders and had almost died a few months prior.

This really affected me knowing that the effects of the torment in school was still affecting her to this day and had ruined her life. She was judged and bullied just because of her body size!

I often think back to school and wish I would have had the courage to twat fuck out of that bully as now with hindsight and other events it transpired that he was just some cowardly little shit who wasn't hard at all (Obviously).

So raise your kids with this in mind as it can literally destroy someone.

Take what you will from this folks and have a good week.

As The Peoples Artist it's my job on a Monday morning to remind you that cheats never prosper.

When I was a kid in school we had a rabbit (Thumper) in class that we all looked after. During the 6 weeks holidays a draw was held to see which kid got to look after the rabbit over the holidays. I love animals but I was only ever allowed to own terrapins so I saw my opportunity and seized it. For the draw the teacher gave us all a scrap of paper to write our name on so I decided whilst no one was looking to tear other pieces of paper from my school book so I increased my chances of winning and when the hat came around I put them all in folded up small (My name was in the draw 11 times).

Much to my delight, the powers of mathematical probability meant I won (Obviously) and I got to take the rabbit home. All was well till a week before the end of the 6 weeks holidays when the neighbour's cat killed the rabbit. I knew if I told my mum she would go ballistic so I buried the rabbit and used my saved-up pocket money to go buy another (All white rabbits look the same).

I returned to school and took Thumper back and all was well for about 2 weeks when one day another kid was shouting excitingly for us all to come look as Thumper the male rabbit had given birth to 5 baby rabbits! I was clearly busted and had to confess to the teacher who saw the funny side of it and never told my mum about it. So, the moral of the story is to still cheat folks but just make sure you've covered every base.

Take what you will from this folks and have a good week.

As The Peoples Artist it's my job on a Monday morning to remind you that sometimes we are our own problems but that also means we are our own solutions.

I'm back on the sober trail for a while after having a little bit too much fun the past year. As much as I will miss ale I'm glad I won't miss the days when I'm mistaking the taxi driver's meter for the time and requesting instead of being took home I'm requesting being took back to the pub. No more late-night YouTube discos drunken doggie dancing with my dog who stands on its hind legs and I hold its paws dancing and laughing my head off around the kitchen (Bit disturbing actually). No longer will I have dreams of diffusing bombs and awaken to find I've cut the plug of the alarm clock. No more Naked drunkenness in the garden singing Jesus Christ Superstar – HOSANNA, no more waking up in the wrong field at festivals, no more crazy drunken Ebay purchases (A pillowcase with Henry Winkler's face on), no more phoning in sick to work telling them I'm wankered and won't be in.

So folks I'm not telling you it's going to be easy but it's going to be worth it.

Take what you will from this folks and have a good week.

As The Peoples Artist it's my job on a Monday morning to remind you that as childhood shows the man, as morning shows the day.

I was sat thinking the other day that growing up and losing all the wondrous things of childhood can never be recovered in the same manner. The joy of running home to watch Grange Hill, collecting conkers, drawing in your school book, making the transforming noise when playing with transformer toys, collecting wood for bonfire night and eating tomato sauce butties. I did however come to this conclusion whilst sat in my cardboard castle I had made.

When we were kids our mum would bath us in the kitchen sink, which was always a great thing to do so last week when no one was home, I stripped off and climbed into the sink. Being a 39 year-old and not a 3-year-old this had clearly changed somewhat over time. Due to my obvious size in comparison to the sink I created a vacuum and my arse was wedged tight in the sink and it's safe to say that I won't be trying that again. Nostalgia isn't what it used to be.

However, last night I was transported back to the 12-year-old me, the one that burnt down the Blackpool Fun House (The Statue of Limitations is up now). I was sat at my table with Parksy's Art World Sticker book franticly turning the pages and putting in the stickers. Accidentally putting the sticker of me in the wrong place I felt like a kid again.

I'm off out now to ride my Chopper and burn down some fun houses.

Take what you will from this folks and have a good week.

As The Peoples Artist it's my job on a Monday morning to remind you that there is a fine line between genius and insanity.

A mate of mine was sectioned once after a drug induced bout of psychosis and was put on a psychiatric ward for a little while to recover.

One time when I was visiting him we were just sat chatting and one of the other in-patients came over and asked if we wanted to play a game of pool. I obviously looked perplexed as there was no pool table in sight but seeing my mate smiling and encouraging me to was play I reluctantly agreed.

The other patient says let's play for money and suggests a fiver, once again I'm puzzled but agree as my mate nods and the other patient goes and selects an invisible pool cue off the invisible rack and then proceeds to arrange the invisible balls on the invisible pool table into the triangle.

At this point I don't know what the fuck is going on as he says he will break first and then goes through the motions of going around the imaginary table potting balls. "See, I'm good at this aren't I? I've never lost to any of the lads" he says.

I'm sitting there with my mate and I haven't a fuckin clue what's going on but my mate explains that he does this to all the other patients on the ward robbing fivers off them, but they give it to him because they feel sorry for the guy as he clearly isn't compos mentis.

Me and my mate continue to watch this guy go around the imaginary table potting every invisible ball and when he says "I won, where's my fiver?".

I think fuck this so I say… "It's there on the table mate"

Take what you will from this folks and have a good week.

As The Peoples Artist it's my job on a Monday morning to remind you that procrastination is the thief of time.

If like me you have the greatest intentions of making your masterpiece but find yourself distracted by cats that play the piano on YouTube now is the time to kick this procrastination and to get busy. My list of planned projects and things to do keeps getting bigger each day and spending time on social media is only prolonging the starting of these tasks. I say let's all make plans for projects we intend to do and make a vow to start them as a year from now you may wish you had started today. So, heed these words, it's what you will actually do that counts not what you intended to do.

Take what you will from this folks and have a good week.

As The Peoples Artist it's my job on a Monday morning to remind you that bureaucracy is a system that enables ten men to do the work of one.

Every day, a small Ant arrived at work early and started work immediately, she produced a lot and she was happy. The Chief, a Lion, was surprised to see that the ant was working without supervision. He thought if the ant can produce so much without supervision, wouldn't she produce more if she had a supervisor? So, the Lion recruited a cockroach who had experience as a supervisor. The cockroach's first decision was to set up a clocking in attendance system. He also needed a secretary to help him write and type his reports. He recruited a spider who managed the archives and monitored all phone calls.

The Lion was delighted with the cockroach's report and asked him to produce graphs to describe trends so that he could use them for presentations, so the cockroach had to buy a new computer and recruit a fly to manage the IT department. The Ant, who had been once so productive and relaxed, hated this new plethora of paperwork's and meetings which used up most of her time. The lion decided to nominate a person in charge of the department where the ant worked. The position was given to the Ladybug whose first decision was to buy a carpet and an ergonomic chair for her office. The new person in charge the Ladybug, also needed a computer and a personal assistant, who she had brought form her previous department to help her prepare a work and budget control strategic optimization plan.

The department where the ant works is now a sad place, where nobody laughs anymore and everybody has become upset, it was at that time the Ladybug convinced the boss, The Lion to start a climatic study of the environment. Having reviewed the charges of running the ant's department the lion found out that the production was much less than before so he recruited the Owl a prestigious and renowned consultant to carry out an audit and suggest solutions. The owl spent 3 months in the department and came out with an enormous report, in several volumes, that concluded that" The Department is overstaffed."

Guess who the lion fired first? The Ant of course "Because she showed lack of motivation and had a negative attitude."

Take what you will from this folks and have a good week.

There are some irresponsible twats out there!

As I was driving to work some idiot, head down on their mobile not looking where they were going steps right out into the road causing me to slam the brakes on.

I spilt my beer fuckin everywhere!

As The Peoples Artist it's my job to remind you that your worst humiliation is only someone else's momentary entertainment.

Last week I attended a manager meeting and all went well with the week finishing on a high. However, on the Saturday I spotted my jacket that I had worn to the meetings on my coat rack with something hanging off the hood. I got closer and realised it was a pair of my boxer shorts stuck to the Velcro of the hood.

Dread then set in. I had washed my coat before the meetings and they had stuck to the Velcro and id travelled on a train for 2 hours with countless people seeing them and then been in meetings with managers for hours. Oh the humanity…Id had my underwear hanging from my jacket hood whilst acting all professional and talking statistics etc. I have to see these people again shortly… world swallow me now.

Take what you will from this folks and have a good week.

As The Peoples Artist it's my job on a Monday morning to remind you that it's better to feel pain than nothing at all.

There was once a child born to a King and Queen and visitors travelled from afar to bring gifts. A wise old Wizard came and granted them one quality to bestow upon the child. They asked the Wizard that he never feel pain so he could go through life the happiest he could be and how he would grow up to be a loving and caring King.

The Wizard pleaded that they pick a different quality which angered the king and queen as they couldn't understand why. The Wizard reluctantly granted their wish and left the kingdom hastily.

20 years past and the Wizard returned one day to see the kingdom in ruins. He found the old King and Queen disheveled and broken. They said they couldn't understand why he had grown this way as he had become a tyrant overlord, waging war and destroying innocent villages and communities.

The Wizard simply explained that as he didn't feel nothing he did not know the pain and suffering of others. It is this pain in life that helps us to feel how others feel and makes us compassionate people.

Take what you will from this folks and have a good week.

As The Peoples Artist it's my job to remind you that the least questioned assumptions are often the most questionable.

I've carried some nuts assumptions with me in my lifetime. It was only 3 years ago that I stopped washing our clothes twice in the machine. Once for a full cycle with washing powder then again with a full cycle for softener, I assumed everybody did this, can you imagine what our electric bills were like and the embarrassment when I found out what we were doing was not the norm.

I also thought that Jimmy in Quadrophenia had died at the end because of the scene of the scooter going over the cliff. I remember someone telling me he throws his scooter off the cliffs and walks back home as he is disillusioned with the movement and it went against the years of what I thought was the ending.

The biggest assumption Id carried since a kid was that the song "I saw mummy kissing Santa Claus" was about a slut of a mum that the kid had witnessed cheating with Santa. Lo and behold, it turns out that Santa is the kid's dad dressed up and is kissing his wife.

Take what you will from this folks and have a good week.

As the Peoples Artist it's my job on a Monday morning to remind you that if something doesn't feel right then it probably isn't.

When I was a kid about 8 years old Id slept at my Nans house and got up early and dressed myself. My Nan woke up and made my breakfast and saw that I'd dressed myself and assumed everything was ok and took me off to school. In school it became apparent something wasn't quite right in the underwear department as I was losing circulation there. I was uncomfortable all day and continually readjusting. When I got home and told my mum my undies were too tight and I stripped off, my mum suddenly burst out laughing. It transpires that I had mistaken a pair of my relative's knickers for a pair of Y-Fronts and I'd been wearing proper ball strangler knickers all day in school.

Suffice to say I'm glad they were of the uncomfortable nature or my choice of lifestyle could have turned out a lot different and remember folks if something doesn't feel right, turn left.

Take what you will from this folks and have a good week.

As The Peoples Artist it's my job on a Monday morning to remind you that lightning can strike twice.

A lad I once worked with has, to coin a phrase from my work wife "The Devils Arsehole". The toilets are off limits for about an hour after he's dropped bombs. Well anyway one day he was in working on his own and he needed to take a slam. As he was finishing someone was repeatedly knocking at the door which he assumed was a client so rushing from the toilet he opens the door and I can only imagine to the shock on his face as he saw it's PHS, the Sanitary Disposal lady come to pick up the Jam-Rag bin from the bathroom.

He was mortified as she braved going into the toilet, he cringed as he heard her flushing the toilet and couldn't sign the sheet fast enough to get rid of her. When he told me the story I pissed myself laughing at it as the next time she came at 7:30 am and carded us just to avoid coming.

The following month he is in the toilet again and there's a knock on the door and you should have seen the smirk on my face when I saw it was the PHS lady again. I asked could she come back but she said she couldn't so she stood waiting outside the toilet door. Out comes my colleague again, she sees its him again and for a second contemplates saying I will come back. She goes in for the second time and I'm thinking if she isn't out in 20 seconds we will go in and rescue her. She comes out doesn't ask for anything to be signed and bolts out the door, she has never returned to our office since.

Take what you will from this folks and have a good week.

I just invented a new word...

Plagiarism

As the Peoples Artist it's my job to remind you at Christmas that sometimes it's best to go without and be together than to try and have and to be apart.

When I was a kid my parents in all their wisdom decided to pull an insurance job on our house at Christmas time. I obviously wasn't aware of this so one night after being at my Nan's my mum and me went home to find the house completely and utterly trashed. Even though my mum was in on it my dad had done that mad a job of making it look authentic that my mum was utterly devastated and was in complete shock crying her eyes out. The house looked like a bomb had hit it and I'm surprised he never went as far as to write, "*I will be back*" in human shit on the walls.

I know deep down their intentions were good but the manner they did it in totally ruined my Christmas. It was only later in life I learnt the truth and probably my greatest lesson, which was why this year I informed our daughter of our intentions and she duly agreed to write on the wall in shit. Granted she's getting a new Apple iPad this year.

Take what you will from this folks and not only have a great week but have a Cracking Christmas.

As The Peoples Artist it's my job to remind you that you only live once but if you do it right then once is enough.

As the end of the year draws to its end (That's an artist joke) I have been reflecting upon the past year and just how much of a buzz it's been and how much was accomplished during it. This year I've climbed mountains (Literally) and have shared lots of great experiences with so many amazing people, old friends and new. I have been overwhelmed and touched at times by those that have told me how much my friendship means to them which is honestly and sincerely reciprocated.

I have so many great memories from this year alone that if I was to die today I'd go a happy man, even the messed-up ones are funny like me missing my flight to the Spain SSOSVA exhibit (I'm such a knob!). There's far too many of you for me to mention but I'd like to thank everyone that is a part of my life and may we continue onward and upwards together.

Take what you will from this folks and have a Happy New Year.

As The Peoples Artist it's my job on Monday morning to remind you that trusting your intuition can save you from shit.

When I was a kid one winter when I was at school I'd been given the task of ringing the school bell for break time so after walking the corridors and ringing the bell I was a few minutes ahead of everyone else in getting out into the playground. I had stood by the doors waiting for my friends to come out when for no apparent reason something inside me told me to not wait and to go out into the empty yard, I'm not sure what I was thinking at that time except a compulsion to just do it.

After Id got a few yards away I heard an almighty cracking sound and then the smell of human shit filled the air. I turned around and man there was shit absolutely everywhere, all up the walls, solitary turds on the floor, little gangs of brown meanies, everywhere. It looked like a stool massacre.

The toilet block was above the door entrance and the pipes to the toilet trailed from there and along the outside walls. The cold had frozen the pipes and exploded launching excrement everywhere.

I had escaped forever being known as 'Poo Boy' by something in my head warning me to move away. I thoroughly enjoyed watching people's reaction when they walked out the door and the wall of shit and stench hitting them. I still giggle to this day at the sheer horror on people's faces at the sight of so much human shit up the walls and on the floors. Truly the stuff of legend when you are 10 years old.

Take what you will from this folks and have a good week.

As The Peoples Artist it's my job on a Monday to remind you that the true sign of intelligence is not knowledge but imagination.

Albert Einstein used to attend a lot of speaker's dinners, which he found weary, as he really wanted to be doing his lab work. One night as they were driving to a dinner, Einstein mentioned to his chauffeur that he was tired of speechmaking. The chauffer resembled Einstein somewhat and having heard Einstein's many speeches proposed that he pretend to be Einstein and give the speech. Einstein thought this was hilarious and agreed to do it.

When they arrived, Einstein put on the chauffeur's cap and jacket and sat at the back of the room. The chauffeur gave an almost perfect rendition of Einstein's speech and even answered a few of the audience's questions. Then an up-his-own-arse professor asked an extremely odd question about the motion of molecules, attempting to flex his intellectual muscle. As quick as a flash the chauffeur stared out the professor and replied "Sir, the answer to that question is so simple that I will let my chauffeur, who is sitting in the back, answer it for me."

Take what you will from this folks and have a good week.

Ruin a Bands Name with 1 letter

I'll start it off with Blue Oyster Cunt

As The Peoples Artist it's my job on a Monday to remind you that not every artist is a media hungry fame obsessed egomaniac (Except me).

Unbeknownst to most people, artists who choose pseudonyms and wish to remain anonymous do not do so because they think it's "cool". I have never met any artist that has chosen this option and most have very valid reasons due to the nature of their employment, their friendships with high profile artists or just their disdain of societies 15-minutes of fame obsession. Most people I know would dread any fame, recognition from their peers yes, but fame…no.

I am somewhat honoured and privileged to know that a majority of the artists with pseudonyms entrust me with a lot of real-world information about them. They do this because they know I not only respect the unwritten rule but also, I have massive respect for them and their privacy. Remember folks there is no kudos in revealing you know artists real names to other artists it just basically makes you look a cunt and untrustworthy.

Take what you will from this folks and have a good week.

As The Peoples Artist it's my job on a Monday morning to remind you that one's dignity may be assaulted and mocked but it can never be taken away unless it is surrendered.

When I was a teenager I hung out at my mates to watch videos and play Mario. His older brother was cool but his mates were absolute stoner knobs and would just be total bell ends to us making cunts out of us all the time.

Me and my mate decided to get them back once so we had recorded about an hour's worth of TV adverts on to VHS and when they were round next stoned we put it on. After about 20 minutes of adverts I could sense their heads were starting to wobble so that's when me and my mate went into the kitchen and swapped t-shirts. Naturally none of them wanted to say they were going white so they all sat in silence, their faces were priceless.

Sensing they were all wobbled I then gave one of them a little blue bookie pens with a rizla cigarette paper rolled around it and watched him try to light it for about 2 minutes.

After that my mate changed the time on the clock in the dining room and commented how time was dragging. I've never seen a collective of people on a whitey before and suffice to say for some reason they chose not to get stoned there again and left me and my mate alone somewhat like Pavlov's Dog one might say.

Take what you will from this folks and have a good week.

As The Peoples Artist it's my job on a Monday morning to advise you not to wait for the perfect moment but to seize the moment and to make it perfect.

They say that good things come to those that wait but sometimes you wait patiently on life's treadmill clutching and grasping and regretting the chances that you never took. To quote Helen Keller "Life is either a daring adventure or nothing at all" so to embark on that adventure, when you want something you've never had before you have to do something you've never done before. It is taking those risks and grabbing hold of those moments that make life what it is and having you wondering why you didn't do it sooner.

So remember folks Qui Audet Adipiscitur and have a good week.

As The People's Artist it's my job on a Monday morning to remind you that revenge is a dish best served cold (Or in my dogs case steaming hot).

The past week my house has resembled what my imagination of The Osbourne household is. Not the drink or the drugs but the smell of dog shit. It's been a shock for me as I've have had our dog Zuki for 9 years and although it's an old stinky dog she's never once shit or pissed in the house. I can understand the new dog (Mika) is a pup and needs training but I'm figuring it as much a shock to our old dog as it is to us. (Contrary to popular belief I only find the look of dog shit hilarious, the smell sends me insane).

That's why I took immense joy when we came home the other day and our dog Zuki took 3 massive shits in my daughter Baby Bill's room. It was a calculated and coordinated attack with strategic target points which obviously took much thought and planning from Zuki. I was so proud of my dog for this well thought out revenge attack and it showing the young pup who was still the boss of the house.

Take what you will from this folks and have a good week.

Today's Peoples Artist Post has been cancelled due to wet leaves on the tracks.

As The Peoples Artist it's my job on a Monday morning to remind you that while we are free to choose our actions, we are not free to choose the consequences of our actions.

A few weeks back I sold a painting for a friend and I deposited the money in his bank but for a laugh I thought I'd write the reference as Refund - Fonda Cox Escorts. My friend thought this lowbrow humour was hilarious and we both had a bit of giggle over it.

Fast forward to this week and I get a concerned phone call from my friend as he had just had murder with his missus. They were visiting a mortgage broker and needed 3 months bank statements so you can imagine the horror when he had to explain a few grand entering his account as a refund from an escort agency. I'm not sure if he is allowed to play out with me anymore as this is a long line of incidents involving my name.

Take what you will from this folks and have a good week.

PS - And don't ask me to transfer money into bank accounts for you.

As The Peoples Artist it's my job on a Monday morning to remind you that sometimes you can't see what's right in front of you.

A few years back me and my mate was so pissed off our tits and was going to another mates of ours. I thought it would be hilarious to knock and drop my pants so when he answers the door I'm just stood there like its normal.

A bit of back story is that his folks were elderly and never answered the door but can you imagine the horror when on this one occasion his 80-year-old mum answers. I'm stood there with kecks round ankles debating about how to proceed so in my wisdom I decide to just carry on as normal as if nothing was out the ordinary. Turns out my mate was out the pub so I'm stood there for 5 minutes chatting to his mum and not once does she even realise my pants are down. After she shut the door I slowly pulled them up and turned to my mate and went WTF.

Take what you will from this folks and have a good week.

As The Peoples Artist it's my job on a Monday morning to remind you we are each our own devil and we make this world our own hell.

I often mentally hear the line from Pink Floyd's Wish you were here "SO YOU THINK YOU CAN TELL HEAVEN FROM HELL" and whenever I'm having too much fun and misbehaving I'm often heard muttering the phrase "I'm going to hell!". However, I had an epiphany the other day thought what if I've been such a good boy previously that this life is now my reward and all the fun shit and shenanigans is my reward.

Whilst some of us are out doing the fun shit and shenanigans (Our heaven) there are others that would like to make their version of their heaven your hell to which we won't succumb. We are our own Gods and we must rule our own heaven or own hell.

Take what you will from this folks and have a good week.

As The Peoples Artist it's my job on a Monday morning to remind you that a friend knows all your good stories but a true friend has lived and shared them with you.

This past week has shown me just how lucky I am to have such a supportive, positive and creative group of friends within my life. Over the course of the past few years I've been lucky enough to have amazing times with incredible people, which I will cherish forever. Some of these friends you don't get to see that often but when you do its always such a happy vibe it's as if time knows no distance. For this I am eternally grateful.

Take what you will from this folks and have a good week.

I just got some new aftershave that smells of breadcrumbs, the birds love it.

As The People's Artist it's my job on a Monday morning to remind you that what you think you know may not always be right.

A few of you are aware that in the past I washed everything twice in my household in the washing machine because I assumed this is what everyone did. Once with washing powder then again with fabric softener. It took some convincing when someone told me that no one else in the world does this and what I'd been doing it the past 20 years was mental.

The other week at my Aunties, Disney's Bambi was on and my 3-year-old cousin referred to Bambi a boy (Not the street artist). I'd always thought since I was a kid that Disney's Bambi was a girl and to be told by my cousin and Auntie that my 30 yearlong belief was wrong was a bit of a shock. However, I asked a few other people who also told me that they thought Bambi was a girl so I feel somewhat less traumatised now. (Please no one shatter my illusion that Bambi Street artist isn't really some hot chick though). My point is what your think, hear or read may not always be the truth.

Take what you will from this folks and have a good week.

As The Peoples Artist it's my job on a Monday to remind you that a sharp tongue can cut your own throat.

I have a very good friend from way back that I don't see that often who I love hanging out with. He had a bit of a fall out with his wife and came to mine for a pre-pub drink and a bit of a whinge. Whilst at mine his phone goes and it's his missus so he takes it in the garden and comes back all pissed off saying they've broken up. Being a good friend that he is to me I proceed to make him feel better by totally trash talking her for ages and he just sits there not saying anything.

This carried on like this for about 20 minutes when I have a paranoid moment and say to him, make sure your phones off. He picks his phone up off the table, looks at it, puts it to his ear and just says "You heard all that didn't you"!

He had only gone and left his phone on and not disconnected the call he took in the garden so his missus heard everything we'd said. I totally burst out laughing and could only mutter the words "Classic". I took him the pub and got him smashed and kept his spirits up by throughout the night bursting into laughter and muttering "Classic". All's well that ends well though as they sorted it all out however he is not allowed to play out with me anymore. (We still will though)

Take what you will from this folks and have a good week.

As The Peoples Artist it's my job to remind you that the only way to rid of temptation is to yield it.

I can resist almost anything except temptation and with the good vibes and the sun at the weekend I gave in and had a drink because going to a pub and having a coke is like going to a prostitute for a hug. My time away from them showed me how much I missed Morgan telling me "Trust me…. you can dance" and Jack saying, "Your awesome at Karaoke, get up and sing". I know I only lasted a week but drinking is not as bad as people make out, it contains some nutrition and vitamins but you just have to drink shit loads of it to benefit, I think this may be along similar lines as cannabis cures cancer.

So, I say give in to temptation and do what thou wilt shall be the whole of the law.

Take what you will from this folks and have a good week.

(Just no murdering any prostitutes).

As The Peoples Artist it's my job on a Monday morning to remind you that nothing worth having was ever achieved without effort.

We live in an I want it now generation with everything being spoon fed to us. If everything was easy in life then we would all be doing it, it takes time, effort and resources to achieve anything of any merit. Things don't just appear, you have to keep going and persevere, as effort will only release its reward after you refuse to quit.

Take what you will from this folks and have a good week.

As The Peoples Artist it's my job on a Monday morning to remind you that men have feelings too (For example we mostly feel thirsty for beer).

It's been claimed that I am in fact a computer programme wrote in the 1960's but I'd like to deny that rumour and state that I am an actual real person with real life issues and feelings. I am not a robot, however once in Amsterdam whilst off my tits I convinced myself I was a transformer. If you hit me; it hurts (I almost like it) if you cut me I bleed (And faint coz I'm a pussy). I am a simple person with a complicated mind, but a person none the less, I am not Jack's lack of emotion. I'm off to relax in a bubble bath with some candles whilst chanting "His name is Robert Paulson".

Take what you will from this folks and have a good week.

As The Peoples Artist it's my job on a Monday to remind you that some people enter our lives as blessings, others as lessons.

A very dear and important friend (My work wife) once told me that people enter our lives for a reason which being a man of science at the time was totally alien to me. However, it became apparent that this was in fact true and we both had come into each other's lives at the time we both needed each other. This person taught me many lessons and made me a better and stronger person and together we rode out some tough times. Some come into our lives to teach us, others to heal us, some to love us and some hate us. Only you will know eventually what that person entered your life for.

"People come into your life for a reason, a season or a lifetime. When you figure out which one it is, you will know what to do for each person"

Reason, Season, Lifetime - Author Unknown

Take what you will from this folks and have a good week.

As The peoples Artist it's my job on a Monday to remind you that in life's movie some days you're the main star, others you're just the bit part actor.

When I was younger I was told a story by a mate of mine. His mate was in a bar and was approached by an attractive woman and a very skinny nerdy man. She asked if he would like to go back to theirs to have sex whilst the husband watched. He was freaked out at first but thought if the man was to kick off he looked like he couldn't punch a hole in a wet paper bag so he agreed to go back to theirs.

He went back to theirs and whilst at the deed the man just sat in the corner watching but was furiously peeling an orange (I didn't understand that part either). The whole thing was getting unnerving and the women didn't seem to be getting into it. After he climaxed he wanted to get out of there sharpish and as he was getting dressed the nerdy guy was starting to get undressed and he had the biggest cock the lad had ever seen.

He made his exit sharpish and as he was going down the stairs he said he heard laughing which still haunts him to this day.

It was the realisation that he was merely the warm-up fluffer in this bizarre sexual encounter and the skinny guy was the main attraction. Oh the humanity.

Take what you will from this folks and have a good week.

As The Peoples Artist it my job on a Monday morning to remind you to take pride in how far you have come and have faith in how far you can go.

A very good friend of mine recently decided to quit the art scene and after wishing him well he texts me "I hope you get all you want". I thanked him but it wasn't until I reflected upon this that I realised that I already have got all I wanted. I have been thinking the past few days just how far a lot of us have come the past few years. If everything was to stop tomorrow I would die a happy man, I am immensely proud of all that's been achieved so far.

We've all embarked on a journey that to be honest I don't know entirely where it may take us. I'm just along for the ride however I do know that a few of the determined few will go far. Our journey is only just starting and hopefully many others will join us for the ride and just who knows how far we will go! So, if you are reading this and haven't embarked on your journey yet, then hop aboard and join the ride.

Take what you will from this folks and have a good week.

Just watched a documentary on Minimalism

It was 4 hours long.

As The Peoples Artist it's my job on a Monday morning to remind you that things aren't always as they seem, the first appearance deceives many.

When I was a teenager I was out and about and called my girlfriend to tell her what time I'd be home. Whilst on the phone I asked her what she was doing and she said she was out with Sandy, a girl from college who I'd met once before. Whilst on the phone to my girlfriend I'm chatting away and I spot Sandy on the other side of the road, minus my girlfriend. My mind crashed, I asked again where she was with Mandy and she said were just leaving college. I thought in my mind she's lying because she is probably out cheating on me. I never said nothing and let it eat at my mind for a few weeks then one day whilst out with my girlfriend we bumped into Sandy who unbeknownst to me has an identical twin who was with her and they were basically cloned replicas of each other. It occurred to me that I had seen the twin out the previous weeks and my girlfriend wasn't lying.

Take what you will from this folks and have a good week.

As The Peoples Artist it's my job on a Monday morning to remind you not to worry about people stealing your ideas or designs, worry about the day they stop stealing them.

When I was younger I submitted some designs to a certain toy company that made robots that transformed. I got the usual bullshit response and forgot about it. About 9 months later I was a bit miffed when I saw my submitted design but altered enough times to not warrant it mine anymore. It happened with a training shoe company also who in the end I told them to fuck off and missed a good opportunity. It's happened to me with a TV script and I couldn't watch a certain TV show for years because I was so pissed off and the worst was a very famous artist who stole a lot of my ideas/designs of me in a rather sneaky manner also.

Whilst it is annoying it shows that your mind is sharp and your ideas are good and one day you may get to shit from a high onto these very people.

Take what you will from this folks and have a good week.

As The People's Artist it's my job to remind you that life's not all plain sailing.

In life we often embark on journeys of which we don't know the end destination. Sometimes (or in my case, mostly) they're aboard a ship with no captain. Even when there is storms and times are scary never abandon ship, sail that boat till you run a ground (Or till you at least sink the fucker). Or perhaps maybe if your determined enough it might just reach its end destination.

Take what you will from this folks and have a good week.

Silent Bill - Chiefs Mate, RMS Titanic

As The Peoples Artist it's my job on a Monday morning to remind you that the trouble with life isn't that there is no answer, it's that there are so many answers.

I've spent all my whole life looking for answers to things that are completely irrelevant in the grand scheme of things. I've literally spent years wasting mental effort on some things that can't be solved and even when solved also aren't even worth knowing the answers*. With the help of friends, I've only just started to be at ease with myself about realising that we cannot know the answers to everything and it's also ok to not know the answers. (Mental tortures a bitch).

I say it's time to let them unanswered questions go from your mind and try not fill your head with new unanswered ones. Google can give you hundreds of answers but only you can give yourself the one right answer.

Take what you will from this folks and have a good week.

The unanswered questions…

*As a child Liverpool had a game abandoned mid-way due to snow etc. Ian Rush scored a goal via a header. The game was abandoned with Liverpool winning 1-0. I never did get to find out the score from the replay.

*I spent a few weeks doing a massive jigsaw only to find at the end of it that the piece was missing, I never did find it but I want to know where the fuck the piece was.

*I watched a sci-fi film as a kid which had a scene in it with a character that looked like Popeye that when he lost a limb he regenerated a whole new identical copy of himself. During a battle scene they regenerate hundreds of this fella to help them to cross some bridge…I'm tortured not knowing the films name (Also people ask am I sure I wasn't on acid and made this up).

*When I was younger we used to record on cassette all manner of daft shit. My uncle recorded something that sounded like gremlins from the movie. The bastard never did tell me how he did it. I suspect it was pop bottle rattled together echoing though.

As The Peoples Artist it's my job on a Monday morning to remind you that you have to be willing to lose everything in order to gain yourself.

Last week I was chatting to a very articulate middle class, middle aged woman who had literally lost everything after a very messy divorce. She was homeless after losing her house, with only 2 years from mortgage ending due to £30k lawyer fees in a custody battle for her kids. It was heart-breaking.

She was in massive rent arrears with council due to the bedroom tax after getting a 3-bed property as she was told she'd need that for custody of her kids. The thing that struck me about her was her positive attitude, even after 2 years of constant shit. She said that it had made her realise what the important things were in life, money was clearly not one of them and how she had found peace with herself and understood herself now as a person. I learned a lot that day from this person.

Take what you will from this folks and have a good week.

As The Peoples Artist it's my job on a Monday morning to remind you to occasionally break the routine so no post this morning.

(What a paradox as I've made the post already).

As The Peoples Artist it's my job on a Monday morning to remind you it's hard to wait for something that may not happen but it's harder to give up when you know its everything you want.

We all have things we want and things we want to achieve. Life seems an endless chase of new goals and new dreams. Sometimes the things we want may seem impossible or out of our reach but my mind says shake that tree till fruit does fall. It's obviously not going to be easy or else it wouldn't be a challenge and things will no doubt get in your way and hinder your dreams.

Regardless of what obstacles are in your way, just keep going, if its people then think the phrase "Haters are my Motivators", if it's a wall, knock it down, if it's a bridge, then build it. Remember folks that a bend in the road is not the end of the road. Keep going with whatever it is you want in life.

Take what you will from this folks and have a good week.

As The Peoples Artist it is my job on a Monday morning to remind you that cheating is a choice not a mistake.

Last week during my weekly beer and card session with God and the Devil I learnt a very valuable lesson. As per usual we were listening to Black Sabbath, drinking beers and playing cards when an argument between God and the Devil ensued. Im used to these fuckers bickering so told them to shut the fuck up but it escalated to God offering the Devil outside for a sorter. Naturally, I knew God would get a proper pasting so I calmed it down, got some more beers and said lets just play cards. All was well for a while when it started again and a kick off was looming, so I suggested playing cards for a soul. Being the drunken tit, that I am I agreed for my soul. Knowing the Devil was my good bud and had my back I was confident all would be well so I dealt the cards and off we went.

We drank, we danced, we swore and we sang along to Sabbath whilst playing cards. The gambling was intense and it boiled down to the last hand. I felt confident by the Devils acknowledging wink that my soul was in safe hands, I knew he had a good hand. God was as usual the arrogant twat, even not bothering to flinch when we told him there was a tsunami happening in East Asia.

It came down to the last hand and God turned over an Ace, King , Queen Jack, Ten. Both me and the Devil looked at each other and knew the twat had us. We saluted him and I honoured the agreement and offered up what was due. God fucked off coz he souls to save elsewhere and me and Lucifer were sat chatting. I asked him what the fuck went wrong, why didn't he sort it and cheat. He said he thought he had God beat as he was sitting on 3 aces… I looked at him and said WTF… how's that possible. I turned over my cards and showed the devil my hand which contained an Ace. We both looked at each other and thought God you cheating Twat.

Take what you will from this folks and have a good week.

As The Peoples Artist it's my job on a Monday morning to remind you that an opportunity not seized upon will be taken by others.

When I was a teenager we had been out all night at a rock club and we had gone back to my mate's house to check out this new thing called the internet he had just got. I told my mate it would never catch on but went along to carry on the party and drink beers.

Whilst he was showing us the wonders of how long it took to load a page on a 56k modem I went for a piss. When I was in the bathroom I spotted my mates super-hot sisters knickers on the bathroom floor (She was super-hot but a right bitch to our mate). The mental turmoil of do I steal them to keep (Bit too extreme for me) or do I steal them for a laugh to show the lads (This seemed a plausible idea). Good sense prevailed and I went down stairs empty handed but I couldn't resist whispering the tale to one of my crazier mates. We sat there for like 2 minutes then he says he needs a piss...I'm thinking he's off to steal them and after a short while he returns back down stairs with a massive smile on his face. He sits silent for a minute then leans over to me and whispers "go look in the bathroom".

I made my excuses and headed to the bathroom, I knew exactly what I was looking for so imagine my horror when I walk into the bathroom and spot the knickers on the floor but now with a massive skid mark in them. My mate had only gone and wiped his arse on them to make out that she had skiddy knickers! I couldn't contain my laughter so imagine my joy when I came down stairs to see everyone giggling away at a cat playing a piano on the internet.

Take what you will from this folks and have a good week.

As The Peoples Artist it's my job on a Monday to remind you that whilst failure is always a possibility, its far worse to never even try to fly.

There is an old tale of a farmer who found an Eagles egg that had fallen from a tree and was still warm. He took it and put it in his chicken coop and eventually hatched. The Eagle spent its life reared and surrounded by chickens and never assumed that itself was in fact an Eagle.

Never witnessing the chickens flying the Eagle lost its ability to fly and grew old on the farm. One day a giant Eagle flew overhead and the Eagle on the farm witnessed it and said to itself

"I wish I was an Eagle and could fly".

Take what you will from this folks and have a good week.

As The People's Artist it's my job on a Monday morning to remind you that you should never judge a book by its cover (Unless it's a porno book).

When I was a kid I liked the wrestling and at the time people sided with either Hulk Hogan or The Ultimate Warrior. I was in the Hogan camp and detested the Warrior, until a few years back. First was the hypocritical steroid saga (So much for taking vitamins eh) then I watched the Hulkster's reality tv show and he was a controlling egomaniac. Now he's been shown to be a racist cunt.

I've since gone back and looked at The Warriors career of sheer intensity and mad ramblings of summoning power within (Hogan chose saying your prayers). And it transpires Warrior was a bit of a nutter but a spiritual one and a family man at that. I was a child at the time so couldn't see through all the bullshit but I'm an adult now.

Take what you will from this folks and have a good week.

As The Peoples Artist it's my job on a Monday to remind you to always be open minded as things aren't always what they seem.

When I was the manager at a job I had to do the recruiting and all the HR stuff. One time during a recruitment process I got back the aptitude and personality tests from the candidates and got the shock of my life. One of the tests said do not recruit this person as they are lazy, unmotivated, self-destructive and will digress easily. Me and a work buddy had a right laugh about this as it was my test.

There hadn't been enough applicants to submit the tests to HR so me and another staff member did one each just to make up the testing numbers. I'm not sure how the test came up with them answers as I was in role and had been doing it with very minor self-destructive things actually going on other than what Id usually do for a laugh like the time I.....Sorry I'm digressing.

Take what you will from this folks and have a good week.

As The Peoples Artist it's my job on a Monday morning to remind you that to live your life you have to risk sticking your head above the parapet from time to time.

I hear people who are always complaining about missing their chances but these are the very people who never take the risks. Unless you're extremely lucky then shit isn't just going to happen, you have to make it happen. Muhammad Ali once said, "He who is not courageous enough to take risks will ACCOMPLISH nothing in life".

If that thing is on your mind that you've been meaning to do, it's still on your mind for a reason. To phrase Shia Lebeauf "Just Do it", as a part of being creative is not being afraid to fail. If you win you will be happy, if you lose you will be wiser.

Take what you will from this folks and have a good week.

Silent Belle's just left me because I'm so insecure…

No wait, she's back, she was just making a cup of tea!

As The Peoples Artist it's my job on a Monday morning to remind you that it is not money that makes our lives rich.

One day a rich dad took his son on a trip to a village to show him how poor some families can be. They spent time on a farm with a poor family. Afterwards the dad asked, "Do you realise what poor is now, what has this made you realise?"

The son said "We have a pool, they have rivers, we have YouTube, they have books, we have one dog, they have four, we buy our food, they grow theirs, we have lights at night, they have stars, we have Facebook, they have real friends, we have stresses, they have none".

The son then said "Thanks Dad for showing me just how poor we are"

Take what you will from this folks and have a good week.

ABOUT SILENT BILL

Silent Bill is an anonymous British Street Artist who has a penchant for vandalising and as self-proclaimed 'Peoples Artist' likes to post random musings.

He is also the founder of the International Arts Collective, The Secret Society of Super Villain Artists or more conveniently and easily known to its many members worldwide as SSOSVA.

When time permits he is also a very proud member of the notorious Brass Monkeys, championing social injustice wherever it may be.

Printed in Great Britain
by Amazon